C000136036

THE UNEXPURGATED ADVENTURES OF
SHERLOCK HOLMES

BOOK 1

A BALLS-UP IN BOHEMIA

by NP Sercombe

The un-edited manuscript originally entitled
A Scandal in Bohemia written by
Dr. John Watson and Sir Arthur Conan Doyle

Illustrations by Emily Snape

This novel is entirely a work of fiction. The names, characters and incidents portrayed in it are the work of the author's and illustrator's imaginations. Any resemblance to actual persons, living or dead, events or localities, is entirely coincidental.

Published by EVA BOOKS 2019 – c/o Harry King Films Limited
1&2 The Barn
West Stoke Road
Lavant
n/r Chichester
West Sussex PO18 9AA

Copyright © NP Sercombe 2019

The rights of Nicholas Sercombe to be identified as the author of this work have been asserted in accordance with the Copyright, Designs and Patents Act 1988.

A CIP catalogue record for this book is available from the British Library.

ISBN 978-1-9996961-0-8 (Hardback)

Book layout & Cover design by Clare Brayshaw.

Cover illustration by Emily Snape.

Set in Bruce Old Style.

Prepared and printed by: York Publishing Services Ltd
64 Hallfield Road, Layerthorpe, York YO31 7ZQ

Tel: 01904 431213

Website: www.yps-publishing.co.uk

All rights reserved. No part of this publication may be reproduced, stored in a retrieval system, or transmitted, in any form or by any means; by that we mean electrical, mechanical, photocopying, recording or otherwise, without the prior written permission of the publisher.

This book is sold subject to the condition that it shall not, by way of trade or otherwise, be lent, re-sold, hired out or otherwise circulated without the publisher's prior written consent in any form of binding or cover other than that in which it is published and without similar condition including this condition being imposed on the subsequent purchaser.

THE UNEXPURGATED ADVENTURES OF
SHERLOCK HOLMES

Books in the Series:

Nicholas Sercombe is a writer and producer for film and television. He has been lucky enough to work in comedy for most of the Holocene period with some of the greatest performers and writers. He is most comfortable when reading Conan Doyle and even happier when re-writing these extraordinarily entertaining stories by Dr. John Watson.

Emily Snape is a coffee addicted, London based illustrator, who's work can be found internationally on books, magazines, the web, television and even on buses.

She studied at Central Saint Martins, Bristol and Kingston and is rarely found without a pencil in her hand. She loves sketching in the streets of London and thinks life is too short for matching socks.

For lovers of Sherlock Holmes who enjoy laughing

A Balls-Up in Bohemia

(published in The Strand in July 1891 as A SCANDAL
IN BOHEMIA *by Dr. Watson and Arthur Conan Doyle)*

To Sherlock Holmes she is always *the* woman. I have
seldom heard him mention her under any other
name. In his eyes she eclipses and predominates the
whole of her sex. It was not that he felt any emotion
akin to love for Irene Adler. All emotions, and that
one particularly, were abhorrent to his cold, precise,
but admirably balanced mind. He was, I take it, the
most perfect reasoning and observing machine that the
world has ever seen; but as a lover, he would have placed
himself in a false position. Throughout the many years
that I knew Sherlock Holmes, he preferred to satisfy
his more basic instincts in a consigned moment and
then move back to his life of detection, without looking
back. He was a one-night-only event, which was usually
impulsive and, therefore, often dangerous. In fact, he
never spoke of the softer passions, save with a gibe and
a sneer. They were admirable things for the observer –
excellent for drawing the veil from mens' motives and
actions. But for the trained reasoner to admit such
intrusions into his own delicate and finely adjusted
temperament was to introduce a distracting factor
which might throw a doubt upon his own high-power
lenses, would not be more disturbing than a strong
emotion in a nature such as his. And yet, there was but

one woman to him, and that woman was the late Irene Adler, of dubious and questionable memory.

I had seen little of Holmes recently. My marriage had drifted us away from each other. My own complete happiness, and the home-centred interests which rise up around the man who first finds himself master of his own establishment, were sufficient to absorb all my attention; while Holmes, who loathed the very form of society with his whole Bohemian soul, remained in our lodging in Baker Street, buried amongst his old books, and alternating from week to week between cocaine and ambition, the drowsiness of the drug, and the fierce energy of his own keen nature. He was still, as ever, deeply attracted by the study of crime, and occupied his immense faculties and extraordinary powers of observation in following out those clues, and to clearing up those mysteries, which had been abandoned as hopeless by the official police. From time to time I heard some vague account of his doings: of his summons to Odessa in the case of the Trepoff murder, of his clearing up of the singular tragedy of the Atkinson brothers at Tricomalee, and finally of the mission which he had accomplished so delicately and successfully for the reigning family of Holland.

A wittier man than myself would say that Holmes was still engaged in the art of *de*-duction whilst I had moved on to the art of *se*-duction! But what may appear to have been the perfect situation was, in truth, a symbiotic disaster. Firstly, all three of Holmes's engagements had taken place over the last fortnight, and so I had missed out on three fantastic adventures that I may have chronicled, along with this adventure, for *The Strand*. Secondly, since I had welcomed my great friend to the day of my marriage to the dear, pretty and beautiful

Mary Morstan, I had made a devastating and terrible discovery about my wife whilst on our honeymoon. In that brief period, I had cut short the holiday and then frittered away the time at home, plucking up the courage to reveal a secret that could only be divulged to my closest friend, instead of standing alongside the great detective to give an honest account of each case *and* be paid to write about it. That was all lost now because, dear reader, merely sharing what is available only in the daily press was too little.

It was on the night of 20th March 1888 I was returning from a journey to a patient (for I had returned to civil practice from the house I had taken with Mary in Queensbury Place, South Kensington), when my way led me through Baker Street. As I passed the well-remembered door, which must always be associated in my mind with my courtship wooing and the dark incidents of the *Sign of Four*, I was seized with a keen desire to see Holmes to reveal the shock discovery about my Mary. His rooms were brilliantly lit, and, even as I looked up, I saw his tall figure pass twice in a dark silhouette against the blind. He was pacing the room swiftly, eagerly, with his head sunk upon his chest, and his hands clasped behind him. To me, who knew his every mood and habit, his attitude and manner told me their own story. He was at work again. He had risen out of his drug-created dreams and was hot upon the scent of some new problem. My yearning was great; my reticence diminished to a level where I was ready to interrupt him and tell him everything.

In anxious trepidation, I rang the bell. The door was unlocked and swung open to reveal Mrs. Turner. I was surprised and disappointed to see her there. We had met before. This was Mrs. Hudson's sister, but she was not the same charming character; in fact, she was quite the opposite. Mrs. Turner wore a face like a wet weekend in Wittering, her flinty eyes were set in teak tissue, like a boxer – the dog, not the sportsman – and punched-dour, with the mouth turned down in a bitter arc. She was one of the most sour-faced bruisers in London. Moreover, she despised all men.

I lifted my bowler. 'Mrs. Turner! How splendid it is to be back here in your sister's most charming house. Is Mrs. Hudson not here this evening?'

'What do you want?' she barked. 'You don't live here no more.' She pointed upwards. 'And he's expecting someone posh. Get out!' She grabbed a broom from inside and tried to sweep me off the doorstep. What followed was an ugly struggle. As she tried to close the door I staved off the preclusion with my shoulder and, eventually, I won the contest. It gave me a chance to think. I puffed myself up to my full five feet and eight inches and locked eyeballs with her.

'Mrs. Turner! I am here to visit my old comrade-in-arms. Now, show me in. Immediately!'

She receded. All she needed was a firm hand, and the army had taught me all about that. She mumbled some indistinguishable mutterings and allowed me a narrow entrance. I squeezed past her over the threshold, close to her craggy chin, whilst removing my hat and delivering a grin. She made no reaction, the jaw steadfast, as if it had been chiselled out of stone from the Mine of Misery. No volume of urging could persuade her to even lift her eyes to mine and give me a smile.

We climbed the staircase together, with me leading the way. She followed with a gradual clomp! clomp! clomp! I could hear her heavy breathing. I could feel

Mrs Hudson's sister disliked men, especially me!

her eyes boring into my backside. As we ascended, I wondered to myself what cruel hand of fate had slapped this poor woman into such a melancholy human being? Was it an unhappy upbringing? Unlikely, because her sister was such a delight. Was it a bad marriage? Maybe… A lost child? Penury? Or was it just sheer bad luck in life?

We reached our destination and she planted herself next to me. 'Thank you, Mrs. Turner, but I can manage from here.' She stayed put. I stared at her loitering. The last thing I wanted was for her to linger and earwig my private revelation to Holmes, so I gave her a dismissive farewell, in army style. She didn't like that at all. She had the gall to return the gesticulation and tell me where to go as well. But she crept slowly away down the landing, so my missive had been acknowledged. I suppose she thought she was in a position of superiority, the building being her sister's property.

I entered the familiar upstairs drawing room. Holmes was hardly effusive. He seldom was; but he was glad, I think, to see me for he was in a jovial mood.

'My dear Watson, it has been so long. We haven't even had the time to change the locks!' With a kindly eye, he waved me to an armchair, threw across his case of cigars, and indicated a spirit case and a gasogene in the corner. Then he stood before the fire and looked me over in his singular introspective fashion. Before I could tell him about my anxiety, he opened the batting.

'Wedlock suits you,' he remarked. 'I think, Watson, that you have put on seven and a half pounds since I saw you.'

'Seven pounds only,' I answered tartly, because I wished to make my confession as soon as possible to remove the weight from my shoulders. 'I say, Holmes, we debate a very trivial matter. There is something much more important that I wish to tell you.'

He was still weighing me up in size. 'Indeed, I should have thought a little more. Just a trifle more, I fancy, Watson.'

'Holmes, it is only seven pounds!'

'And a half. And I observe you are in practice again. You did not tell me that you intended to go into harness.'

'Then, how do you know?'

'I see it, I deduce it. How do I know, for instance, Watson, that you have been getting yourself very wet lately, and that you have a most clumsy and careless servant girl?'

'My dear Holmes,' said I, 'this is too much. You would certainly have been burned at the stake had you lived a few centuries ago. It is true that I had a country walk on Thursday and came home in a dreadful mess; but, as I have changed my clothes, I can't imagine how you deduce it. But this is a sideshow – I have something much more valuable that I wish to tell you.'

He chuckled to himself and rubbed his long nervous hands together. 'I suppose I may have been perceived as a wizard in the Dark Ages. But this servant girl, how come she is still in your employ?'

I made the mistake of dithering before making a response. 'As to Mary Jane, she is incorrigible, and my wife has given her notice.'

'You hesitated, Watson. Are you sure it was your wife?'

'Yes, I am sure, Holmes! Now, I am glad that we have got onto that subject. That is precisely what I came here to discuss with you.'

But he ignored me, for the second time, and steered the conversation back to his deductions, with an air of careless complacency.

'Watson, this maid of yours. It is simplicity itself,' said he.

'The devil, Holmes, I fail to see how you work it out.'

'My eyes tell me that on the inside of your left shoe, just where the firelight strikes it, the leather is scored by six almost parallel cuts. Obviously, they have been caused by someone who has very carelessly scraped round the edges of the sole in order to remove crusted mud from it. Hence, you see, my double deduction that you have been out in vile weather, and that you had a particularly malignant boot-slitting specimen of the London slavery.'

'You are correct. She is a myopic savage! Awful. Now, about my wife ...'

'Do not interrupt, Watson. I wish to tell you how I have deduced that you are back in practice. You see, if a gentleman walks into my rooms smelling of iodoform, with a black mark of nitrate of silver upon his right forefinger, and a bulge on the side of his top hat to show where he has secreted his stethoscope, I must be dull indeed if I do not pronounce him to be an active member of the medical profession.'

I could not help laughing at the ease with which he explained his process of deduction. 'When I hear you give your reasons,' I remarked, 'the thing always appears to me to be so ridiculously simple that I could easily do it myself, though at each successive instance of your reasoning I am baffled until you explain your process. And I believe that my eyes are as good as yours.'

'Quite so,' he answered, lighting a cigarette, and throwing himself down into an armchair. 'You see, but you do not observe. The distinction is clear. For example, you have frequently seen the steps which lead up from the hall to this room.'

'Frequently.'

'How often?'

'Well, this apartment has been my home. It will be some hundreds of times.'

'How many are there?'

'I don't bother to count. My mind is usually set on other things. Let me tell you, when I was ascending the staircase just now, I thought that I was being followed up the treads by the bride of Frankenstein!'

'HOY!' came Mrs. Turner's barking exclamation through the door, now set slightly ajar, from the landing behind me. 'COME HERE AND SAY THAT!'

'Excuse me, one moment please, Holmes.' I rose from my chair. I marched over to the door. I had a clear view of Mrs. Turner nearby as she pretended to polish the mahogany stair rail.

'Mrs. Turner!' I commanded. 'I bade you farewell but here I find you eavesdropping. You are not the bride of Frankenstein; you are the *mother* of Frankenstein. Go away!' I slammed the door shut. I ambled back to my chair and relapsed into it.

'So, how many are there?' asked Holmes.

'How many of what?'

'Steps. How many steps are there on the staircase?'

'How many? I don't know!'

'Quite so! You have not observed. And yet you have seen. That is just my point. You even had the chance to cheat – you could have counted them just now – but you did not. I know that there are seventeen steps, because I have bothered to see, and I have observed.'

'Frankly, Holmes, I couldn't give a monkey's arse how many steps there are. I have much more important issues in my life to consider at the moment, which is why I made the effort to drop in.'

'By the way,' he said, 'since you are interested in these little problems, and since you are good enough to chronicle one or two of my trifling experiences, you may be interested in this.' He threw over a sheet of thick pink-tinted notepaper, which had been lying open upon the table. Blow me down, he ignored my plea yet again! The man was so self-centred he had the gravitational pull of Jupiter. 'It came by the last post,' he continued. 'Read it aloud.'

'No!' I said. 'I have got to tell you something. It is very important. To me, at least.'

'Well, I cannot think of anything more valuable or more of a priority than a new mystery.'

'Holmes!'

'Look at the notepaper, Watson.'

'My revelation is something you could not, and would not, possibly know. And that's because *nobody* knows, except for me!'

'Nobody knows that your wife is a female impersonator?'

I jumped up out of my chair. 'BY GOD, YES, HOLMES! MARY IS A MAN!'

An ear-piercing, high-pitched shriek pierced the musky atmosphere, like a bolt of lightning. Suddenly, Mrs. Turner crashed through the door into the room, her habitually-glum frame doubled-up in heavy laughter, her eyes pouring out tears! We waited patiently but it was no good; she was in a spasm and could not stop herself. It was Holmes who resigned first. He jumped up and bundled her out of the room, with a 'Yes. No. Not a word now. No, not to anyone...' followed by the unmistakable sound of human tissue being slapped hard. It was brutal but necessary, to stem her hysteria successfully. Such treatment is accepted by the medical community throughout the civilised world and Holmes would have aimed his hand well, being the excellent amateur pugilist that he is. Medicine aside, I would have preferred to see his size 10 up her backside! When he had finished, and closed the door behind him, he turned to look at me, his features not declaring the slightest remorse. He picked up our conversation where it had left off.

'You poor fellow,' he said. 'You could not see it. Mary was in an advanced state of gender transformation.'

'Thank you, Holmes. How did you know?'

'I had written a treatise on female impersonators.'

'Of course you had!' I quipped cynically. Then a manuscript entitled *When Man Becomes Woman*, by S.N.J. Holmes, landed upon my lap, which reminded me that sarcasm simply never worked on Sherlock, Nugent, Julius Holmes. I glanced at it and flicked through the pages. It was a proper piece of work, just like its author...

'It was the Adam's apple, not the bricklayer's hands that alerted me,' said he. 'Maybe the oh-so-too-even bosom? Or was it the walk? The sway of the hips, as those of a navy rating after a trans-Atlantic voyage?'

Who would have thought that my dear friend was an expert on gender transition?

That was when the penny dropped – Holmes was chiding me! He was playing me out like an accomplished angler.

'Or the way his periscope went up when she French-kissed me?! Ha! Ha! Ha!' he finished off.

'Please, no more Holmes!'

He couldn't stop laughing, sadly at his own humour. 'Don't feel so bad, Watson!' he said. 'Mary is a professional. He, or she, as I should say, even knows how to disguise her Adam's apple, whether it be by neck-chief, choker or cravat. It took a real detective, such as myself, to calculate the size of the said organ, thus transferring suspicion to deduction. In fact, I have written a short monograph upon the subject, all thanks to you.'

'Oh, really?'

'Yes. Here you go.'

He threw a pamphlet at me, which I caught in my left hand. I sighed. Again, my attempt at sarcasm had been vanquished. I glanced at the front page, the print encircling a copperplate illustration of several Adams apples (various). 'My dear friend, why didn't you let me know?'

'But I did, Watson. I did! How often did I let slip to you that Mary would make a fine baritone, eh? But you never took any notice.'

'You are right, Holmes! But my fiancée was a rare beauty. I thought that your jests were a form of jealousy. I can see now that I should have taken notice. And I should have thought more about the reasons why her father was not interested in giving her away.'

'Why, indeed, that none of her family attended the ceremony?'

I buried my head in my hands. 'My marriage is a sham! There will be an annulment.'

'On what grounds?'

'Non-consummation, of course!'

'That might be tricky to prove. It is likely to get very embarrassing, Watson. I would just pay him off for a divorce on, say, grounds of... unreasonable over-abundance of genitalia?'

I didn't rise. Instead, I was thrown into confusion. What was I to do? For the moment I thought it best to put my problem to one side, but I had to clear up one last item.

'My dear friend, I was just wondering if I could...'

'Yes, you should move back in. Your room is just as you left it.'

I thanked him, with more enthusiasm than I should, but it was out of sheer relief, and he could see that in my demeanour.

'Now you can relax, Doctor. I shall send Mrs. Turner to Queensbury Place to fetch your daily and immediate requirements.'

'No, Holmes!' I ejaculated. 'NOT Mrs. Turner!' But he was laughing already, behind the hand he had thrust out in between us acknowledging a joke stepped on too far.

'I shall send a boy to fetch your things.' And he calmed down. 'Now, this pink notepaper; it came by the last post. Why don't you read it out aloud?'

I took the note. It was undated, and without either signature or address.

'There will call upon you tonight, at a quarter to eight o'clock,' it said, 'a gentleman who desires to consult you upon a matter of the very deepest moment. Your recent services to one of the Royal Houses of Europe have shown that you are one who may be safely trusted with matters which are of an importance that can hardly be exaggerated. This account of you we have from all quarters received. Be in your chamber then at that hour, and do not take it amiss if your visitor wears a mask.'

'This is a mystery,' I remarked. 'What do you imagine that it means?'

'I have no data yet. It is a capital mistake to theorise before one has data. Insensibly one begins to twist facts to suit theories, instead of theories to suit facts. But the note itself. What do you deduce from it?'

I carefully examined the writing, and the paper upon which it was written.

'The man who wrote it is presumably well-to-do,' I remarked, endeavouring to imitate my companion's processes. 'Such paper could not be bought under half a crown a packet. It is particularly strong and stiff.'

'Indeed so, Doctor! But the word I am looking for is "peculiar,"' said Holmes. 'It is not an English paper at all. Hold it up to the light.'

I did so, and saw a large _E_ with a small _g_, a _P_, and a large _G_ with a small _t_ woven into the texture of the paper.

'What do you make of that?' asked Holmes.

'The name of the maker, no doubt, or his monogram, rather.'

'Not at all. The _G_ with the small _t_ stands for "Gesellschaft," which is German for "Company." It is a customary contraction like our "Co." "P," of course, stands for "Papier." Now for the _Eg_. Let us glance at our

"Continental Gazetteer." He took down a heavy brown volume from his shelves. 'Eglow, Eglonitz – here we are, Egria. It is in a German-speaking country – in Bohemia, not far from Carlsbad. Remarkable as being the scene of the death of Wallenstein, and for its numerous glass factories and paper mills. Ha, ha, my boy, what do you make of that?' His eyes sparkled, and he sent up a great blue triumphant cloud from his cigarette.

'The paper was made in Bohemia,' I said.

'Precisely. And the man who wrote the note is a German. Do you note the peculiar construction of the sentence – "This account of you we have from all quarters received." The verb is at the end of the phrase or sentence each time. A Frenchman or Russian could not have written that, and certainly not an Englishman. Only a German is so uncourteous to his verbs. It only remains, therefore, to discover what is wanted by this German who writes upon Bohemian paper and prefers wearing a mask to showing his face.'

Holmes cocked an ear towards the street windows. 'And HERR he comes! Ha, ha ha!'

'What is so funny?'

'It's a joke.'

'Really?' I knew precisely what it was, but I was seeking revenge upon his earlier torment of me. I had no intention of letting him get away with it.

'It's a play on words. "Herr" as in the German for "Mister." Herr he comes, instead of *here* he comes!'

'Oh? Is that it?'

'Yes. That is it.'

'Really? That IS it, is it?'

'Yes! That IS IT, Watson!'

'Well, I suppose that must be it?' Then, annoyingly, I cracked a smile. He caved in quickly.

'Hmm! I suppose I am pleased to see some of the old-style Watson back on show again.'

Outside, there was a sharp sound of horses' hooves.

'It's a pair by the sound,' said he. 'Yes,' he continued, glancing out of the window. 'A nice little brougham and a pair of beauties. A hundred and fifty guineas apiece. There's money in this case, Watson, if there is nothing else.'

'Thank goodness for that. I am going to need some, for this divorce.'

There was a sound of the grating of wheels against the kerb. Holmes whistled. 'Now there's a driver who will be looking for new employment in the morning.'

'I would like to agree with you, Holmes, but anyone is entitled to a minor misjudgement now and again.'

'A shilling says that I am correct, Doctor!' And he withdrew a shiny coin from his waistcoat and chocked it onto the side. I fumbled around for a shilling to match Holmes's and placed it on top.

'I wonder what is going on out there.'

There followed a sharp pull at the doorbell.

'If I am not mistaken, the German has arrived, just in time to resolve all our doubts.'

'Just in time to save us from your awful puns.'

'Do you want me to go out for a while, and leave you to it?'

'Not a bit, Doctor. Stay where you are. I am lost without my Boswell. And this promises to be interesting. It would be a pity for you to miss it.'

'But what about this client of yours? He sounds rather fancy.'

'Fancy is as fancy does, so never mind him. I may want your help, and so may he. Here he comes. Sit down in that armchair, Doctor, and give us your best attention.'

A slow and heavy step, which was followed by that of Frankenstein's mother, had been heard upon the stairs and in the passage, paused immediately outside the door. There was a loud and authoritative tap.

'Come in,' said Holmes.

A man entered who could hardly have been less than six feet six inches in height, with the chest and limbs of Hercules. His dress was rich with a richness which would, in England, be looked upon as akin to bad taste. Heavy bands of astrakhan were slashed across the sleeves and fronts of his double-breasted coat, while the deep blue cloak which was thrown over his shoulders was lined with flame-coloured silk and secured at the neck with a brooch which consisted of a single flaming beryl. His trousers were cut in a continental style, a far cry from Savile Row, and tucked into very fine leather boots finished with solid gold toecaps that extended half-way up his calves, and which were trimmed at the tops with rich brown fur. These completed the impression of barbaric opulence which was suggested by his whole appearance. There was absolutely no doubt in my mind that our visitor was a Johnny Foreigner, and, just as Holmes had indicated, he might be a Squarehead.

He carried a broad-brimmed hat in his hand, while he wore across the upper part of his face, extending down past the cheekbones, a black vizard mask, which he had apparently adjusted that very moment, for his hand was still raised to it as he entered. From the lower part of the face he appeared to be a man of strong character, with a thick, hanging lip, and a long straight chin, suggestive of resolution pushed to the length of obstinacy. In other words, he bore the look of a right difficult sod!

'You haff my note?' he asked, with a deep, harsh voice and a strongly marked German accent. Holmes glanced a wink at me to indicate his prediction was so accurate. 'I told you that I would call,' he continued. He looked from one to the other of us, as if uncertain which to address, and set his eyes upon Holmes. 'You there! Are you aware that one side of your face iss red *und* swollen? What has happened to you?'

I hadn't dared comment upon the savage damage that had been inflicted earlier on the great detective by Mrs. Turner's iron fist. Indeed, our visitor was innocent of Holmes's great prowess as a pugilist. He was running in blind to his terrible sensitivity about Mrs. Turner's ability to breach his guard with a jab from the left and a smart hook from the right. But he was lucky – Holmes needed this commission. He just smiled and cleared his throat.

'Thank you. It is a minor allergy caused by a chigger.'

Pants on fire!

'You haff been chiggered? enquired our esteemed guest. 'What does that mean?'

I interjected: 'Sir, I am a doctor and I can tell you that it is the reaction to the bite of the common dust mite.'

'It causes me no distress,' Holmes lied. 'Pray take a seat. This is my friend and colleague, Dr. Watson, who is occasionally good enough to help me in my cases. Whom do I have the honour to address?'

Our visitor remained standing. 'You may address me as Count von Kramm.'

'Is that so?' remarked Holmes disbelievingly. Our visitor blanched at the tone but let it pass. I could see that it grated harshly against his nature. This man wanted something badly.

'I am a Bohemian nobleman.'

'That aspect, I do believe to be true.'

'It certainly is Mr. Holmes!' He flashed an angry look at us both for a moment. 'I understand that this gentleman, your friend, is a man of honour and discretion, whom I may trust with a matter of the most importance that is extreme! If not, I should much prefer to be with you alone to communicate.'

'I shall get on my way,' I remarked. 'I have people to see; letters to write.' I rose to go, but Holmes caught me by the wrist and pushed me back into my chair. 'It is both of us, or none, sir,' said he. 'You may say before this gentleman anything which you may say to me.'

The Count shrugged his broad shoulders. 'Then I will begin,' said he, 'by first binding you both to secrecy that is absolute for two years. Then, at the end off that time, the matter will be of no importance. At present it is ferry sensitive. It is not too much to say that it is of such weight that it may haff a bad inff-lu-ence upon the history of Europe.'

'I promise,' said Holmes.

'I promise as well' I said, but with my fingers crossed on both hands. How else could I write my chronicles without using this type of invaluable information?

'You will maybe this mask excuse,' continued our strange visitor. 'The august person who employs me wishes his agent to you to be unknown, and I may confess, at once, that this title by which I have just called myself is not my own exactly.'

'I am aware of it,' said Holmes dryly.

'The circumstances are of great delicacy, and every precaution haff to be taken to quench what might grow to be a scandal immense and compromise seriously one off the reigning families of Europe. To speak plainly, this matter implicates the great House of Ormstein, hereditary Kings of Bohemia.'

'I was aware of that too,' murmured Holmes, settling himself down in his armchair, and closing his eyes.

Our visitor stared at Holmes making himself comfortable in the chair, his mouth agape, shocked to the core at the sight of the languid, lounging figure. Holmes slowly reopened his eyes and looked impatiently at his gigantic client.

'Oh, you don't like me sitting down without your bidding, do you, Your Majesty?'

The man jumped in the air in surprise and paced up and down the room in uncontrollable agitation. Then, with a gesture of desperation he tore the mask from his face and hurled it upon the ground. 'You are correct!' he cried, 'I am the King! I cannot attempt to conceal it any longer!'

A king in our apartment? Heavens above! In one shake of a lamb's tail I ejected myself out of my chair and stood to attention, bolt upright, eyes front. 'Sir!'

The King gave me a nod of appreciation. Holmes did not move a muscle.

'Why, indeed?' murmured Holmes. 'That was an easy trap that I set for you: to sit down in front of Your

Majesty, without being given permission, flushed you out like a young pheasant. You simply had to be the King.'

'*Donner und blitzen*! I knew in my heart that I was not an actor. Count von Kramm indeed! I was trying to convince you, Herr Holmes, the reasoner most incisive, and the private detective most energetic in Europe.'

'The *only* private detective in Europe, Your Majesty!' I barked, still standing to attention. From the glare I received in return, I wished that I hadn't said anything. It was bad form to make a correction to a king.

'Ignore him, Your Majesty,' said Holmes.

Thus, from that moment on, His Majesty paid me no attention whatsoever. I stood easy and sat back down in my chair.

Holmes continued: 'In fact, Your Majesty had not even spoken a word, before I was aware that I was addressing Wilhelm Gottsreich Sigismond von Ormstein, Grand Duke of Cassel-Falstein and hereditary King of Bohemia.'

What a mouthful! That's the trouble with royalty; they breed in to one other so frequently that they keep accumulating names.

'Then please take a seat and take the weight off those splendid boots.'

Our strange visitor decided, at last, to take a seat next to Holmes. He passed a hand over his high, white forehead and looked him straight in the eye. 'YOU may call me Big Willie.' He extended a hand to Holmes, who looked him straight back in the eye and took it. 'That is what my friends call me. Please, understand that I am not accustomed to doing such business in my own person. Yet this matter was so delicate that I could not to an agent confide it wiz-out putting myself in his power. I have come from Prague incognito for the purpose only off consulting you.'

'Then, pray, consult,' said Holmes, 'but if Big Willie allows, I would prefer to address a newly-acquainted king in the formal way. You have the floor, Your Majesty...' And he slumped down in his chair for maximum comfort and shut his eyes once more.

'As you wish. The facts are these most briefly: some five years ago, during a visit most lengthy to Warsaw, I made the acquaintance of the well-known adventuress Irene Adler. The name is familiar to you, no doubt?'

'Kindly look her up in my index, Doctor,' murmured Holmes. For many years he had adopted a system of docketing all paragraphs concerning men and things, so that it was difficult to name a subject or a person on which he could not at once furnish information. In this case I found her biography sandwiched in between that of a Hebrew Rabbi and that of a staff-commander who had written a monograph upon the deep-sea fishes. More monographs! No wonder Holmes had catalogued her.

'Let me see,' said Holmes. 'Hum! Born in New Jersey in the year 1858 Contralto – hum! La Scala, hum! Prima Donna Imperial Opera of Warsaw – yes! Retired from operatic stage – ha! Living in London – quite so! Your Majesty, as I understand, became entangled with this young person, wrote her some compromising letters, and is now desirous to get those letters back.'

'Precisely so. But *mein Gott*, how...?'

'Was there a secret marriage?'

'None.'

'No legal papers or certificates?'

'None.'

'Then I fail to follow. If this young person should produce her letters for blackmailing or other purposes, how is she to prove their authentication?'

'There is the writing.'

'Forgery.'

'My private notepaper.'

'Stolen and imitated.'

'My photograph.'

'Bought.'

'We were both in the photograph.'

'Oh, dear! That is very bad.'

'How bad?'

'Very bad! Your Majesty has indeed committed an indiscretion.'

The King looked crestfallen. We looked at one another in a nebula of silence.

'I was mad!' said the King. *'Wahnsinnig!'*

I rolled my eyes in wonder at Holmes, who whispered: 'Insane...'

'FICKEN VERRÜKT!!'

I nodded at Holmes. No translation required!

'Well, quite so Your Majesty! You have compromised yourself most seriously.'

'I was only the Crown Prince then. I was young. I am but thirty now.'

'The virility and stupidity of youth aside, it must be recovered.'

'We haff tried *und* failed.'

'Your Majesty must pay. It must be bought.'

'She will not sell.'

'Stolen, then. We just send in the good Doctor here.'

'Oh, ha ha ha Holmes!' I interjected.

The King stared harder at the great detective, ignoring me, of course. 'Five attempts have been made. Twice my burglars in my pay her house haff ransacked. Once we haff her luggage diverted when she travelled. Twice she has been waylaid. There has been no result.'

'No sign of it.'

'Absolutely none.'

Holmes laughed. 'It is quite a pretty little problem,' said he.

'Little?' said the King. 'It is ferry serious! Wait until you see what is in the photograph...'

'I was rather hoping this wouldn't head towards something that obvious?'

'By the composition we are laid bare. There can be no doubt, Herr Holmes.'

'You Germans! You have no shame!'

The King laughed a little. 'Ja, it is true, that we are less reserved than you Englishmen, but in this composition, we are fully clothed. It is the intimacy which is obvious to see. And we Germans think nothing of placing an old dog in a photograph. To us, it makes no difference.'

'It makes sense to me,' I said. 'After all, Miss Adler is an actress. Being an actress conjures a euphemism for prostitute. Being a prostitute makes her a tart. Tart is a euphemism for old dog.'

'*DUMBKOPF!* Fraulein Adler is not any off those insults!' shouted the King now animated and pointing at me. 'I am meaning *my* old dog! My hunting mastiff. "Merkel!" She is in the photograph. Zo! There is no doubt about the identity of the man. Me! Everybody who is anybody in Bohemia, and beyond, associates that dog *mitt* ME!'

'Yes, Watson, do please try and keep up with Bohemian Society.'

'Herr Holmes, what *is this* fool doing here?'

'Ignore him, Your Majesty.'

'Again?'

'Yes, Your Majesty. May I enquire what Miss Adler proposes to do with the photograph?'

'To ruin me.'

'But how?'

'I am about to be married.'

'So, I have heard.'

'To Charlotte Lothman von Saxe-Meningen, second daughter of the King of Scandinavia. You may know the strict principles off her family? No? She is herself the ferry soul of delicacy. A shadow of a doubt as to my conduct would bring the matter to an end.'

'I understand. But in this doomed situation, Your Majesty, where we have a blackmailer on the loose, would you not have the opportunity to call Miss Adler's bluff, discard this engagement and find a replacement?'

'Diss-card?' exclaimed the King. He fumbled around inside his coat and withdrew a photograph. He projected it forwards, towards us, for our perusal. 'See! Here, the Princess! Zo, Herr Holmes, Herr Doctor – remember, gentlemen, we are men off the world!'

The pose in the photograph portrayed the nude female form, just as God had created, but maybe in a position he never intended to be immortalised in celluloid. Certainly, I hadn't seen such raw perfection of a woman's physiological attributes in such an overt position since I studied gynaecology at medical school. It was enough to make a chap spill his beans!

'By Hefner!' said Holmes, turning his head each way to take in all of the angles that Charlotte Lothman von Saxe-Meningen was flexible enough to have delivered.

'The Princess seems to enjoy showing off her very soul of delicacy,' I interjected.

'Ignore him, Your Majesty!'

The photograph was whisked away from our view and re-installed into the King's coat.

'She is not worth "diss-carding" Mr. Holmes.'

'No, no! I agree! And what does Irene Adler intend to do?'

'She threatens to send her photograph to her father, the King. And she will do it. I know that she will do it! You do not know her, but she has a resolve of steel. She has the face off the most beautiful of women, and the mind of the most resolute off men. Rather than I should marry another woman, there are no lengths to which she would not go – none.'

'You are sure that she has not sent it yet?'

'I am sure.'

'And why?'

'Because she hass said that she would send it on the day when the betrothal was publicly proclaimed. That will be Monday next week.'

All the girls love a King!

'Oh, then, we have three days yet,' said Holmes, with a yawn. 'That is very fortunate, as I have one or two matters of importance to look into just now. Your Majesty will, of course, stay in London for the present?'

'Certainly. You will find me at The Langham, under the name off Count von Kramm.'

'Then I shall drop you a line to let you know how we progress.'

'Pray do so. I shall be all anxiety.'

'Then, as to money?'

'You have *carte blanche*.'

'Absolutely.'

'I tell you that I would give one of the provinces of my kingdom to haff that photograph.'

'And for present expenses?'

The King took a heavy chamois leather bag from under his cloak and laid it on the table.

'Here iss three hundred of your pounds in gold, and seven hundred off your pounds in notes,' he said.

Holmes scribbled a receipt upon a sheet of his notebook and handed it to him.

'And mademoiselle's address?' he asked.

'Is Briony Lodge, Serpentine Avenue, St. John's Wood.'

Holmes took a note of it. 'One other question,' said he. 'Was the photograph a cabinet?'

'*Jawohl*.'

'Then, good night, Your Majesty, and I trust that we shall soon have some good news for you. And good night, Watson,' he added, as the wheels of the Royal brougham rolled down the street. 'If you will be good enough to call tomorrow afternoon at three o'clock, I should like to chat this little matter over with you.'

'You have got to be kidding, Holmes! We have three hundred pounds in gold and seven hundred in cash, staring up at us from the table. As your doctor, I advise that we put our bodies into a state of wellness and our minds into a composure where we may stimulate the synapses in the brain most effectively for this adventure. I prescribe the immediate spending of some it.'

'You are right, Watson, and I had forgotten about the abrupt flight from your honeymoon. You must be over-wrought.'

'It has been well over a month, my friend,' I replied.

'Then let us pack up here. We shall take our thoughts and our libidos to Mother Kelly's for a thorough reflection upon this illustrious affair.'

Within two minutes, we had flown down the stairs and hot-footed through the front door. We were on our way to Kingly Street.

* * *

The next morning, I made my way down to Queensbury Place. I bore a thick head upon my shoulders, but I had a spring in my step – Mother Kelly had supplied and delivered the catalyst for both in fine, rounded style. First off, I had struggled to pick out the best choice of clothes available from those that the boy had collected from there the evening before and carried north to Baker Street. I had no doubt that "Mary" had been playing a small joke upon me when he had packed the boy's valise with a mixture of smart Sunday attire and a country bumpkin style of tweed more suitable for crawling through the bogs of Sutherland. Dear reader, if you could stretch your imagination to visualise me standing in front of you dressed in a blue worsted suit jacket atop an evening shirt, a dancing bear necktie, propped up with plus-twos made from the Isle of Olay tweed – the rough stuff, chewed by the native womenfolk – and some half-calf socks. Oh, and the whole ensemble topped off with a brown trilby. I attracted more unwanted attention during that walk to South Kensington than Medrano The Clown – boum! boum! – some people even laughing out loud.

The journey was a wasted one, in the respect that I had no patients in my book and Mary had gone berserk. He had wrecked the house. I had been out for the whole night without any prior notice and that was the cause of his temper. He was not worried about my safety; nor was he angry at my absence. No, he thought that I had absconded, maybe even escaped the country and abandoned him. In revenge, he had cancelled all of my appointments, all three of them, and then persuaded himself into a blind rage that led to the upending of all my furniture and the clearing of all the pictures and mirrors from the walls. This led to a frank conversation between us about what the future held. Mary made his position crystal clear: he would sign an annulment and leave me alone forever if I paid him five thousand pounds. I despaired because this was impossible. I could not even imagine earning and retaining such an enormous sum of money over my entire life. I tried to reach a compromise. I fetched all of the money I possessed in the world at that time, a mere forty-five pounds, from the welsh dresser. In my desperation, I placed the vast majority of it on the table and offered for him to take it, in full and final settlement of our affairs. But it was no use. He demanded five thousand pounds for a complete separation.

At three o'clock precisely I was back at Baker Street, but Holmes had not yet returned. Mrs. Turner informed me that he had left the house shortly after my departure at eight o'clock in the morning. I sat down beside the fire, however, with the intention of awaiting him, however long he might be. I was already deeply interested in his inquiry, for, though it was surrounded by none of the grim and strange features which were associated with the two crimes which I had previously recorded, still, the nature of the case and the exalted station of his client gave it a character of its own. Indeed, apart from the nature of the investigation which my friend had on hand, there was something in his masterly grasp of the situation, and his keen, incisive reasoning, which made it a pleasure to me to study his system of work, and to follow the quick, subtle methods by which he disentangled the most inextricable mysteries. So accustomed was I to his invariable success that the very possibility of his failing had ceased to enter into my head.

It was close upon four before the door opened, and a drunken-looking groom, ill-kempt and side-whiskered with an inflamed face, and disreputable clothes, walked into the room. Accustomed as I was to my friend's amazing powers in the use of disguises, I had to look three times before I was certain that it was indeed he. With a nod he vanished into the bedroom, whence he emerged in five minutes tweed-suited and respectable, as of old. Putting his hands into his pockets, he stretched out his legs in front of the fire and laughed heartily for some minutes.

'Well, really!' he cried, and then he choked; and laughed again until he was obliged to lie back, limp and helpless, in the chair.

'What is it?'

'It is quite too funny. I am sure you would never guess how I employed my morning or what I ended by doing.'

'Bravo, Holmes! I am surprised you had enough sap left in you to even climb out of bed after that Bavarian giant last night.'

'By delving into Gerda, the Bavarian Behemoth...'

'And let's face it, Holmes, she was built like a girder!'

'BY GOING GERMAN... I stuck to the task in hand, thus making legitimate use of the King's cash for expenses. Unlike you, Watson, partaking of Essex! And a couple of hours with Gerda helped me to brush up on my German language and it figured significantly the next in preparing my disguise as a rough-sleeping down-and-out.'

'My dear Holmes, you look suitably exhausted. You wouldn't have needed much make-up! And today, I suppose that you have been watching the habits, and perhaps the house of Miss Irene Adler?'

'I have, but the sequel was rather unusual. I will tell you, however, I left the house a little after eight o'clock this morning, in the character of a groom out of work.'

'Oh, that's what you were? I thought you were a chimney sweep *in* work!'

'Oh, ha ha Watson! I was dressed just like a groom because there is a wonderful sympathy and freemasonry amongst horsey men. Be one of them and you will know all that there is to know.'

'About horses?'

'No, Doctor, about the seven wonders of the ancient world! I soon found Briony Lodge. It is a bijou villa, with a garden at the back, but built out in front right up to the road.'

'Oh dear! I am not sure I would like to be *that* close to a main road, Holmes.'

'How fortunate, then, that you are not living at Briony Lodge! Tell me, Watson, have you had a testing day?'

'I have had a mare of a day, Holmes! Mary spiked my emergency wardrobe that he gave to your boy yesterday. I looked like an explosion at a dressing-up party for my walk south this morning. When I arrived at home, and I had donned my consulting suit, I found that my surgery diary for the day was empty. This was strange because it had been full of patients the day before. I deduced it could only have been Mary that had put them off. I went upstairs to our bedroom only to be assaulted by the sight of Mary packing her bags *au natural*, which he was doing quite deliberately. He wished to cause me emotional distress.'

'Oh! So, everything was on display?'

'The whole fruit and veg department, Holmes. Everything! I could not look at him in that state of undress. The memories of our moments of intimacy kept flashing through my mind. I am a man of medicine, but my true love for him... her... him, is still deeply ingrained in my heart.'

Holmes was in a state of deep pontification, no doubt. Then, his features changed, and he raised his eyebrows mischievously. 'Was the intimacy very intense?' he whispered mockingly.

I stared at him. How could my friend test my sense of humour so earnestly?

'I'd rather not say anything, Holmes.' I thought about that moment again until a chill ran up my spine. I sighed. Holmes nodded, still keeping up the pretence.

'And then he asked for money,' I remarked.

Holmes brightened up. He sat up smartly in his chair. 'Because he was leaving?' he enquired.

'Yes, it certainly looks that way, Holmes. I gave him money.'

'All you had?'

'Every penny, and I told him that it was so. It was about forty pounds, and a couple of old shirt buttons.' I smiled at him.

'Really? He settled on that? Is that all?'

'Oh yes, Holmes,' I fibbed.

'Then you have done well, Watson. Very well!'

He believed me! My word, I knew that I had been fortunate enough to escape lightly from his scrutiny but now that I had the confirmation I sought from the great deducer I was elated. I jumped up and shook his hand saying: 'Indeed so, my friend? Then I am in the clear?!'

'If not a little queer,' he shouted, 'after that experience!' He stood up and clapped his hands on my shoulders. We laughed and laughed. 'That is the last you will ever see of Mary Morstan,' said Holmes. 'Or more-of-Stan? Ha! And now I can see that you are, in fact, in a very good mood. I understand why you are interrupting my account with those silly snipes of yours!'

'Pray, continue your account, Holmes, that I might also continue my sniping!' We laughed again and collapsed back into our chairs. 'So, you had just arrived at Briony Lodge.'

'I remember. I made a brief survey. The villa was not very secure. It has a Chubb lock to the door. There is a large sitting room on the right side, well-furnished, with long windows almost to the floor, and those preposterous English window fasteners which a child could open. Behind the house there was nothing remarkable, save that the passage window could be reached from the top of the coach house. I walked round it and examined it closely from every point of view, but without noting anything else of interest.

'I then lounged down the street, and found, as I expected, that there was a mews in a lane which runs down one wall of the garden. I lent the ostlers a hand in rubbing down their horses, and I received in exchange twopence, a glass of half-and-half, two fills of shag tobacco and as much information as I could desire about Miss Adler, to say nothing of half a dozen other people in the neighbourhood in whom I was not the least interested, but whose biographies I was compelled to listen to.'

'And what of Irene Adler?' I asked.

'Oh, she has turned all the men's heads in that part. She is the daintiest thing under a bonnet on this planet. So, say the Serpentine Mews, to a man. She lives quietly, sings at concerts, drives out at five every day, and returns at seven sharp for dinner. Seldom goes out at other times, except when she sings. Has only one male visitor but sees a good deal of him. He is dark, and dashing; never calls less than once a day, often twice.'

'Twice a day is normal for dashing men of our age. Biologically speaking, that is.'

'Thank you, Doctor, but please don't interrupt. The visitor is Mr. Godfrey Norton, of the Inner Temple. Note the advantages of a cabman as a confidant, Watson! They had driven him home a dozen times from Serpentine Mews and knew all about him. When I had listened to all that they had to tell, I began to walk up and down near Briony Lodge once more, and to think over my plan of campaign.'

'And what did you come up with?' I asked, in great anticipation.

'Wait for it, Watson! Ha! Well, I decided that this Godfrey Norton was evidently an important factor in the matter. He was a lawyer. That sounded ominous. What was the relation between them, and what was the object of his visits? Was she his client, his friend, or his mistress? If the former, she had probably transferred the photograph to his keeping. If the latter, it was less likely. On the issue of this question depended whether I should continue my work at Briony Lodge or turn my attention to the gentleman's chambers in the Temple. It was a delicate point, and it widened the field of my inquiry. WAKE UP WATSON! I fear that I bore with you with these details?'

I shook myself back to reality. I have to confess that my mind had wandered into some vivid images from the night before, of Barbara, 23, from Braintree, all *déshabillée*, stretching herself out tight over the vaulting horse. I pretended to regain my attention and feigned a yawn. 'I am sorry, Holmes, but it has been a long day.'

'AFTER a long night, Doctor! Our deductions lie in the details, so thank you and good night Miss Barbara, 23, of Braintree, and safe journey home. PAY ATTENTION WATSON!'

'I am awake, Holmes, I promise.'

'AT BRIONY LODGE... I was still balancing the matter in my mind when a hansom cab drove up to the house, and a gentleman sprang out. He was a remarkably handsome man, dark, aquiline, and moustachioed.'

'Steady, Holmes. Now I am getting quite hot under the collar!'

'This had to be the man of whom I had heard. He appeared to be in a great hurry. He shouted to the cabman to wait, and brushed past the maid, and walked through the open door with the air of a man who was thoroughly at home.

'He was in the house about half an hour, and I could catch glimpses of him, in the windows of the sitting room, pacing up and down, talking excitedly and waving his arms. Of her I could see nothing. Presently he emerged, looking even more flurried than before. As he stepped into the cab, he pulled a gold watch from his pocket and looked at it earnestly. "Drive like the devil," he shouted, "first to Gross and Hankey's in Regent Street, and then to the Church of St. Monica in the Edgware Road. There's a guinea if you do it in twenty minutes!"

Away they went, and I was just wondering whether I should not do well to follow them, when up the lane came a neat little landau, the coachman with his coat half buttoned, and his tie under his ear, while all the tags of his harness were sticking out of the buckles. It hadn't been pulled up before she shot out of the hall door and into it. I only caught a glimpse of her at the moment, but she was a lovely woman, with a face that a man might die for.'

'Or risk a royal wedding for,' I interjected.

'She cried out: "The Church of St. Monica, John, and half a sovereign if you reach it in twenty minutes."'

'This was quite too good to lose, Watson. I was just balancing whether I should run for it, or whether I should perch behind her landau, when a cab came through the street. The driver looked twice at such a shabby fare; but I jumped in before he could object. "The Church of St. Monica," said I, "and half a crown if you reach it in twenty minutes." It was twenty-five minutes to twelve, and of course it was clear enough what was in the wind.

My cabby drove fast. I don't think I ever drove faster, but the others were there well before us.'

'What do you expect, my dear friend, when the others offered sovereigns and you a mere half a crown? You are tight, sir!'

Holmes gestured a disdainful glance in my direction, and then continued.

'Anyway... The cab and the landau with their steaming horses were in front of the door when I arrived. I paid the man and hurried into the church. There was not a soul there save the two whom I had followed, and a surpliced clergy man, who seemed to be expostulating with them. There were all three standing in a knot in front of the altar. I lounged up the side of the aisle like any other idler...'

'Or passing chimney sweep!'

'Any other idler, or visitor, who just may have dropped into a church to worship, *that being what churches are for, Watson*. Suddenly, to my surprise, the three at the altar faced round to me, and Godfrey Norton came running as hard as he could towards me.

"Thank God!" he cried. "YOU will do. Come on!"

"What for?" I asked.

"Come, man, come, only three minutes or it won't be legal."

'I was half dragged up to the altar, and before I knew where I was, I found myself mumbling responses which were whispered in my ear, and vouching for things of which I knew nothing, and generally assisting in the secure tying up of Irene Adler, spinster, all-round beauty, to Godfrey Norton, luckiest bachelor lawyer in the world. It was all done in an instant, and there was a gentleman thanking me on one side and the lady on the other, while the clergyman beamed on me in front. It was the most preposterous position in which I ever found myself in my life, and it was the thought of it that started me laughing just now. It seems that there had been some informality about their licence, and the clergyman absolutely refused to marry them without a witness of some sort, and that my lucky appearance saved the bridegroom from having to sally out into the streets in search of a best man. The bride gave me a sovereign, and I mean to wear it on my watch-chain in memory of the occasion.'

'How very Braintree of you, Holmes!'

'Yes. If only I wore an ankle-bracelet instead of a watch-chain.'

'But what a very strange turn of affairs,' said I. 'And what then?'

'Well I found my plans very seriously menaced. It looked as if the pair might take an immediate departure, and so necessitate very prompt and energetic measure on my part. At the church door, however, they

Irene Adler tried to see through Holme's fantastic disguise.

separated, he driving back to the Temple, and she to her own house. "I shall drive out in the Park at five as usual," she said as she left him. I heard no more. They drove away in different directions, and I went off to make my own arrangements.'

'Which are?'

'Some cold beef and a glass of beer,' he answered, ringing the bell. 'I have been too busy to think of food, and I am likely to be busier still this evening. By the way, Doctor, I shall want your cooperation.'

'I shall be delighted.'

'You don't mind breaking the law?'

'Don't we do that every time we go out on an adventure together?'

'Yes, but how about the chance of being arrested?'

'I do not mind if it is in a good cause.'

'Oh, the cause is excellent!'

'Then, I am your man.'

'I was sure that I might rely on you.'

'But what is it you wish? What do you have in mind? Have you formulated a plan?'

'When Mrs. Turner has brought in the food and drink I will make it clear to you.' And he rang the bell again. Twice.

'Holmes, if Mrs. Turner is still *in loco officium* to Mrs. Hudson, I suggest you do not upset her by ringing that bell again...'

But Holmes had no time to answer. The door was kicked open. A scowling Mrs. Turner stood in its frame holding a tray laden with meat and ale.

'WHICH ONE OF YOU NOBS KEEPS PULLING THAT BLOODY CORD?' she shouted. Her eyes pounced upon mine with murderous intent. 'YOU!' she cried, and she marched in with purpose, as if her life depended upon its delivery, so much so that we both jumped up to assist her. I lunged forwards and cleared a space on the chiffonier, opening the very top drawers and sweeping in the cocaine crystals, the syringes and the accoutrements, and jamming them shut. Holmes did his bit. He removed heaved-off boots, discarded books and unwanted clutter to make a clear passage from door to table. I just had time to step to one side as she hove into my space and slammed the tray down onto the top of the chiffonier.

'There! This should make you fart!' she shouted, 'I am off. GET OUT OF MY WAY!'

I made the mistake of moving away from the wall, to give myself more space, but this interfered with her swinging around to make her a clear passage towards the door. She stuck her elbows out, quite deliberately, and clocked me a sharp jab in the fleshy part of my arm, deadening the feeling with great pain. Before I could utter a word, she had swung her spare arm around, and her hand grabbed me by the wing of my collar. She hoisted me up in one, swift movement and pulled me towards her face. 'Do you want to make something of it, DOCK-TOR?' And before I could shake my head, she was at me again. 'DO YOU?!'

'No, no, no Mrs. Turner! Here, please take something for your troubles.' I held up a crown, all that I had left after "Mary" had cleaned me out, and the ruse worked well. She used her collar-grabbing hand to swipe the coin out of my clasp. I slumped down, relieved, as Holmes made a deft sideways move to avoid Mrs. Turner. She wrenched the bell cord from its fastening and left the room. Then, he ambled over and stretched out his hand to mine to heave me up on my feet.

'Thank you, Holmes. That was an unpleasant experience. If there is any chance of violence on this mission, may I suggest we invite Mrs. Turner to join us?'

Holmes laughed and turned hungrily on the simple fare that our landlady's sister had provided. 'Maybe we should, Watson! Let us discuss it while I eat, for I have not much time. It is nearly five now. In two hours' time we must be on the scene of the action. Miss Irene, or Madame, rather, returns from her drive at seven. We must be at Briony Lodge to meet her.'

'And what then?'

'You must leave that to me. I have already arranged what is to occur. There is only one point on which I must insist. You must not interfere, come what may. You understand?'

'I am to be neutral?'

'To do nothing whatsoever. There will probably be some unpleasantness. Do not join in. It will end in my being conveyed into the house. Four or five minutes afterwards, the sitting room window will open. You are to station yourself close to that open window.'

'Yes?'

'You are to watch me, for I will be visible to you.'

'Yes! And then what?'

'When I raise my hand – like so – you will throw into the room what I give you to throw, and will, at the same time, raise the cry of "fire!" You quite follow me?'

'Entirely.'

'This is what you will throw. It is nothing very formidable,' he said, taking a long cigar-shaped roll from his pocket. 'It is an ordinary plumber's smoke rocket, fitted with a cap at either end to make it self-lighting. Your task is confined to that. When you raise your cry of "fire!" it will be taken up by quite a number of people. You may then walk to the end of the street, and I will rejoin you in ten minutes. I hope that I have made myself clear?'

'Yes! I am to remain neutral, to get near the window, to watch you, and, at the signal, to throw in this object, then to raise the cry of "fire" and to await you at the corner of the street.'

'Yes, but you will have to raise your voice, Watson. That was pathetic.'

'Oh? How about this? "FIRE!"'

'You sound like an old woman mewing about her arthritis!'

I knew that I could do much better. I had been a chorister at school! I stood up, so that I may give my lungs a chance of full inflation. I took a very deep breath. Then, I let it go!

"FI-RE! FII-AARRE!! FIIIAAAAAAARRRRRR-RR-E!!!!"

I could see that I was making an impression upon my critic. I walked around the room with my arms held out wide, like an opera singer in plight, shouting: "FIII-AAAAARRRRRR!!!! FIII-AAAAAAARRRRRRRR-E!!!!"

Once I was exhausted, Holmes smiled. 'Sit down, Watson. That was excellent, but we don't need the amateur dramatics or to disturb the emergency services with a false alarm.'

'Oh piffle, Holmes! Nobody can hear us up here. Anyway, your plan sounds like a winner. You may entirely rely on me.'

'Yes, you have embraced the strategy with gusto, Watson. Now, I think perhaps it is almost time that I prepared for the new role I have to play.'

'WAAARRRDROO-OOBE!'

'That's enough of that, Watson!' he shouted, and gave me that stern, crooked seagull look that commanded respect, but with humour.

He disappeared into his bedroom. I sat down and listened to my heart thumping away with excitement in my breast. My goodness, this afternoon should bring some colour to our lives!

Holmes returned a few minutes later in the character of an amiable and simple-minded Nonconformist clergyman. His broad black hat, his baggy trousers, his white tie, his sympathetic smile, and general look of peering and benevolent curiosity, were such as Mr. John Hare alone could have equalled. It was not merely that Holmes changed his costume. His expression, his manner, his very soul seemed to vary with every fresh part that he assumed. The stage lost a fine actor, even as science lost an acute reasoner, when he became a specialist in crime.

* * *

It was a quarter past six when we left Baker Street, slightly later than we had planned. We were frustrated by Mrs. Turner's gibes from the building threshold as we stood on the pavement paying off the fire brigade for their wasted visit. With Holmes acting the part of a simpering clergyman, this could only be made in an over-friendly manner. I kept my peace, otherwise he would harp on about his having to give Captain Flack and his firemen five pounds for my robust rehearsals – you will remember, no doubt, that I had been cleaned out by my wife and our prize-fighting housekeeper. It took a long time. We had a deadline to meet and we had to catch up or the plan would fail. We rushed, in an unseemly way, which upset Holmes in the universe of his ecclesiastical character – he insisted that a man of the cloth would always walk, never run. I had to persuade him to cadge a lift on the fire engine.

It was ten minutes to the hour when we found ourselves in Serpentine Avenue. It was already dusk; and the lamps were just being lit when we paced up and down in front of Briony Lodge, waiting for the coming of its occupant. The house was just such as I had pictured it from Sherlock Holmes's succinct description, but the locality appeared to be less private than I had expected. On the contrary, for a small street in a quiet neighbourhood, it was remarkably animated. There was a group of shabbily dressed men smoking and laughing in a corner, a scissors-grinder with his wheel, two guardsmen who were flirting with a nurse-girl, and several well-dressed young men who were lounging up and down with cigars in their mouths.

'You see,' remarked Holmes, as we paced to and fro in front of the house, 'this marriage rather simplifies matters. The photograph becomes a double-edged weapon now. The chances are that she would be as averse to its being seen by Mr. Godfrey Norton, as our client is to its coming to the eyes of his Princess. Now the question is: where do we find the photograph?'

'Where, indeed, Holmes? I have no doubt that you have observed and deduced.'

'I have. It is most unlikely that she carries it about with her. It is a cabinet size. Too large for easy concealment about a woman's dress. She knows that the King is capable of having her waylaid and searched. Two attempts of that sort have already been made. We may take it then that she does not carry it about with her.'

'Where then?'

'Her banker or her lawyer. There is that double possibility. But I am inclined to think neither. Women are naturally secretive, and they like to do their own secreting. Why should she hand it over to anyone else? She could trust her own guardianship, but she could not tell what indirect or political influence might be brought to bear upon a businessman. Besides, remember that she had resolved to use it within a few days. It must be where she can lay her hands upon it. It must be in her own house.'

'But it has been twice burgled.'

'Pshaw! They did not know how to look.'

'But how will you look?'

'Mighty stupid if I cannot crack this!'

'Not even a professional burglar like yourself, Holmes?'

'Oh, ha ha, Watson. I shall get her to show me.'

'Well, good luck, Holmes! She is bound to refuse.'

'She will not be able to. But hark! I hear the rumble of wheels. It is her carriage. Now, do not forget to carry out my orders to the letter.'

As he spoke, the gleam of the sidelights of a carriage came around the curve of the avenue. It was a smart little landau which rattled up to the door of Briony Lodge. As it pulled up, one of the loafing men at the corner dashed forward to open the door in the hope of earning a copper but was elbowed away by another loafer who had rushed up with the same intention. A fierce quarrel broke out, which was increased by the two guardsmen, who took sides with one of the loungers, and by the scissors-grinder, who was equally hot upon the other side. A blow was struck, and in an instant the lady, who had stepped from her carriage, was the centre of a little knot of flushed and struggling men who struck savagely at each other with their fists and sticks. Holmes dashed into the crowd to protect the lady; but just as he reached her, he gave a cry and dropped to the ground, with the blood running freely down his face. At his fall the guardsmen took to their heels in one direction and the loungers in the other, while a number of better dressed people who had watched the scuffle without taking part in it, crowded in to help the lady and to attend to the injured man. Irene Adler, as I will still call her, had hurried up the steps; but she stood at the top with her superb figure outlined against the lights of the hall, looking back into the street.

'Is the poor gentleman much hurt?' she asked.

'He is dead,' cried several voices.

DEAD?!!! My heart leapt into my mouth.

'That is much worse!' she opined, brilliantly. I gazed in wonder as her whole, gorgeous frame shook with shock and she clasped her hand to her bosom; the left one, I think. But what was *I* to do? My friend had told me to stick to his orders, to the letter, but now he was dead. Surely his plan – the plan he had never divulged to me the precise details of – had come undone? I could not hold back any longer. I dashed forwards from my point of observation into the crowd of onlookers shouting 'I am a doctor! Make way for the doctor!'

I dashed in from the right and crouched over the body slain. Holmes's eyes were closed and his whole physique appeared lifeless. I lifted his wrist and felt for a pulse. There was life! I moved in closer, and lent forwards to place my forefingers upon his neck, to check for the same. Definite life! And then Holmes's body went into a spasm, his left leg jerking up, his knee hitting me square in the small of my back. There was a gasp from the group gathered around us, with some lunatic shouting: 'Look! See how the spirit has flown from his body!' When his leg had fallen back to the ground his body was, once again, lifeless. I had been projected forwards and was sprawled across his head. As I gathered myself up, I heard him whisper: 'For God's sakes, stick to my orders! Get me into the house!' His voice was as strong as an ox.

I stood up. 'No, no, no, there's life in him,' I shouted. 'But he will be gone before I can get him to hospital.'

'He's a brave fellow,' said a woman. 'They would have had the lady's purse and watch if it hadn't been for him. They were a gang, and a rough one, too. Ah, he's breathing now.'

I took control of the situation by staring straight at Irene Adler. 'He can't lie in the street. May we bring him in, marm?'

'Surely. Bring him into the sitting room. There is a comfortable sofa. This way, please.'

Slowly and solemnly he was borne into Briony Lodge, and laid out in the principal room, while I stuck to Holmes's plan and stayed outside, in a location where I could observe proceedings from a post by the window.

The lamps had been lit, but the blinds had not been drawn, so that I could see Holmes as he lay upon the couch. I watched as Irene Adler made sure that Holmes was comfortable and then she spotted me. She hurried out of the room and then back onto the front porch. She hailed me.

'Doctor! Surely you will be coming into the house as well?'

This was a fine turn out of events. The devil! I didn't know what to say or what to do!

'Come along! Hurry now...'

I responded in an autonomic way: I walked towards her. I had no choice. Firstly, I am an army person, and I am used to obeying orders. Secondly, I was stuck in such a position where my refusal would have been perceived suspicious. Thirdly, I was a red-blooded male who could never spurn the request of a pretty woman. Did I mention that Irene Adler was a pretty woman?

When I arrived, she delivered a gorgeous smile of such warm intensity that a bolt of electricity shot through my eyes and bounced off my perineum. I gulped as she took me by the arm and walked me inside and around the corner into the sitting room. She went straight over to Holmes and made a fuss of him. He gave me a very hard stare, a style of glare that normally turns the recipient into a rock, or a bag of salt. Or, maybe a bag of rock salt? I do not know whether he was seized with compunction at that moment for the part he was playing, but I know that I never felt more heartily ashamed of myself in my life than when I glanced at the beautiful creature against whom I was conspiring, or the grace and kindliness with which she waited upon the injured man. And yet it would be the blackest treachery to Holmes to draw back now from the part which he had entrusted to me. I hardened my heart and took the smoke rocket from under my ulster. After all, I thought, we are not injuring her. We are but preventing her from injuring another.

Holmes sat up upon the couch and groaned. Irene Adler made even more of a fiddle about him. Once she had her back turned to me, I saw him motion like a man who is in want of air. A maid was instructed to rush across and throw open the window. At the same time, I saw him raise his hand, and, at the signal, I pulled the ignition cord and tossed my rocket across the room with a cry of "FII-AAA-RRRRE!" The word was no sooner out of my mouth than the whole crowd of spectators outside, well dressed and ill – gentlemen, ostlers and servant maids – joined in a general shriek of "FIRE!" I was ready to execute the task that the great detective had set me.

"FIIIRRRRE! FIIIII-YAAAR!" I bellowed. Outside, I could hear the onlookers shout louder. I warmed to their response. I splayed my feet and my arms wide apart and drew in as much breath as I was able. I pushed my pelvis forwards and gave it everything I had, like Puccini with a lightning rod stuck up his Rondine.

"FIIII-AARRR! F..F...F...FIIII-YAAR! GRRR!... GRRR...GREAT FIII-YAARRRR!!"

Thick clouds of smoke curled through the room, and out of the open window. I caught a glimpse of rushing figures, and a moment later the voice of Holmes from within, assuring them that it was a false alarm. Tripping around the room, coughing like a barking dog, I made my way to the corner of the room, and a minute later was rejoiced to find my friend's arm in mine He guided

The army didn't teach their surgeons how to handle explosives.

me away from the billowing smoke. Soon we were out the front door and slipping through the scene of uproar outside. He walked swiftly and in silence for some few minutes, until we had turned down one of the quiet, narrow streets which lead towards the Edgware Road. We stopped on the tiny pavement by a quaint house in a well-lit street. We caught our breath. Holmes drew out a cigarette and lit it.

'In the end you did it very nicely, Doctor,' he remarked. 'Nothing could have been better. It is all right.'

'You have the photograph?'

'I know where it is.'

'And how did you find out?'

'She showed me, as I told you she would.'

'I am still in the dark.'

'I do not wish to make a mystery,' said he, laughing. 'The matter was perfectly simple. You, of course, saw that everyone in the street was an accomplice. They were all engaged for the evening.'

I have to confess that I didn't have even the slightest inkling. 'Oh yes, Holmes, of course I could see that.'

'Then, when the row broke out, I had a little pig's blood in the palm of my hand. I rushed forward, fell down, clapped my hand to my face, and became a piteous spectacle. It is an old trick.'

'Pig's blood? I think that I would have used paint.'

Holmes gave me a brief stare of incredulity. Then, re-assumed the bearing and stance of his clergyman character by standing up straight and peering through his half-spectacles down at me. 'Thou shalt not doubt the methods and means of the Lord Holmes, Doctor,' he preached, 'or use second-rate props.'

'No. Forgive me, reverend, I have sinned. Pray, continue.'

'Bless you, my son.' He gesticulated the sign of the cross over me and re-assumed his true persona with a puff on his cigarette. 'So...then they carried me in. She was bound to have me in. What else could she do? And into her sitting room which was the very room which I suspected. It lay between that and her bedroom, and I was determined to see which. They laid me on a couch, I motioned for air, they were compelled to open a window and you had your chance.'

'How did that help you?'

'It was all-important. When a woman thinks that her house is on fire, her instinct is at once to rush to the thing which she values most. It is a perfectly overpowering impulse, and I have more than once taken advantage of it. In the case of the Darlington Substitution Scandal it was of use to me, and also in the Armsworth Castle business. A married woman grabs at her baby – an unmarried one reaches for her jewel box. Now it was clear to me that our lady of today had nothing in the house more precious to her than what we are in quest of. She would rush to secure it. The alarm of the fire was admirably done. The smoke and shouting was enough to shake nerves of steel. She responded beautifully. The photograph is in a recess behind a sliding panel just above the right bell-pull. She was there in an instant, and I caught a glimpse of it as she half drew it out. When I cried out it was a false alarm, she replaced it glanced at the rocket, rushed from the room, and I have not seen her since. I rose, and, making my excuses, escaped from the house. I hesitated whether to attempt to secure the photograph at once; but the coachman had come in, and he was watching me narrowly, it seemed safer to wait. A little over-precipitance may ruin all.'

It was at that moment we had to postpone our conversation. The level of noise had risen from complete tranquillity to a cacophony of bellringing and men shouting. It was off in the distance but approaching rapidly. We both looked down the street and watched the many brave fellows of the fire brigade running up the cobbles towards us at full tilt, all surrounding the fire engine pulled by four sturdy horses. As they got near to us, there was a severe clanging of the brass bells, so loud that one couldn't hear oneself speak. There was precious room to spare in such a narrow road. We were forced to stand back, our bodies pressed hard against the railings of the quaint house, as the melee of burly fire fighters clattered by. Then, a voice shouted out from above us: 'YOU AGAIN?!' We looked up to see Captain Flack in his lofty position, standing on top of the engine, pointing his finger and looking directly at us.

'YOU!' he shouted. 'PUT THAT CIGARETTE OUT!'

And then, unfortunately, his voice faded away into an echo of emergency heading towards Briony Lodge. We re-organised ourselves back to our original positions on the pavement.

'And now, what do we do, Holmes?'

'Our quest is practically finished. I shall call with the King tomorrow, and with you, if you care to come with us. We will be shown into the sitting room to wait for the lady, but it is probable that when she comes, she may find neither us nor the photograph. It might be a satisfaction to His Majesty to regain it with his own hands.'

'And when will you call?'

'At eight in the morning. She will not be up, so that we shall have a clear field. Besides, we must be prompt, for this marriage may mean a complete change in her life and habits. I must send a wire to the King without delay.'

We walked back through the streets of London, stopping off on the way at a couple of public houses for some refreshing ale and stout. Then, we made a brief diversion south, for a freshener at Mother Kelly's, our credit still being good there, and caused hilarity to the staff and clientele that a clergyman was indulging himself amongst them. So, it was very late in the evening when we reached Baker Street and had stopped at the door. Our tiredness wouldn't cope with Mrs. Turner's sense of humour, so we didn't knock on the door. Holmes was searching his pockets for the key, when someone passing said:

'Good night, Mister Sherlock Holmes.'

There were several people on the pavement at the time, but the greeting appeared to come from a slim youth in an ulster who had hurried by.

'I've heard that voice before,' said Holmes, staring down the dimly lit street. 'Now, I wonder who the deuce that could have been?'

* * *

I slept badly that night. I couldn't work out how the great detective would flush out the photograph without causing a fuss and forcing Irene Adler to escape town with her precious cargo. It finished with a change of scene completely in which Barbara, 23, from Braintree, escorted Irene Adler to the gymnasium, softly, hand-in-hand. I awoke with a raging morning discomfort. But it was only when I opened my eyes that I could understand why I had been dreaming of that liaison. There, crouching beside my bed, was the angel known as Mrs. Hudson, her cheerful face smiling down at me. whilst she offered a cup of fresh coffee with one hand and a good morning with the other.

'Here's a nice surprise,' she said, 'seeing you back here, John.'

'MRS. HUDSON!' I ejaculated. 'You angel, how lovely it is to see you.'

'Likewise, I am sure, Doctor,' she replied. 'I am pleased to see you back.'

'You have brought me coffee. And great happiness.'

'I have missed you,' she cooed, and left the room quietly.

A few minutes later, Holmes and I were engaged upon our toast and more coffee when the King of Bohemia dropped by, as had become his wont. He rushed into our room.

'You haff really got it?' he cried, grasping Sherlock Holmes by either shoulder, and looking eagerly into his face.

'Not yet.'

'But you haff hopes?'

'I haff hopes.'

'Then, come. I am all impatience to be gone.'

'We must have a cab.'

'No, my brougham is waiting.'

'Tell me, Your Majesty,' I asked, 'do you have the same driver as yesterday?'

'No, I had to let him go.'

'Ha!' cried Holmes, who stood up triumphant and marched over to the sideboard to scoop up the two shillings.

'What iss occurring here, gentlemen?' asked the King.

'Yesterday, we had a small difference of opinion, Your Majesty, about...'

'Ignore him!' cried Holmes. 'Come! Let us move onto the final act of our adventure together.'

We descended the stairs. In the hallway, we were obliged to mingle with Mrs. Turner as she too was departing and saying farewell to her sister.

'Goodbye, Mrs. Turner,' said Holmes. 'Send my best wishes to the working girls on the hard standings of Tobacco Docks.'

She swung around all angry and mean, looking as if she may lunge at him. Instead, she placed her fingers on his chin where it had been swollen but was now just slightly inflamed. She locked her eyes on his and stroked the bruised tissue, for what seemed like an hour. Mrs. Hudson could be heard whispering 'now please don't, Elsie...' Then, Mrs. Turner cocked her head at the great detective, smiled and winked at him. Holmes grimaced and opened the door.

'Come, Villie,' he said to the King. 'We should not tarry more than necessary.'

'*Zehr güt* Herr Holmes!' said the King, and he marched out of the door.

'And cheerio, Mrs. Turner,' I said. 'Don't do anything I wouldn't do.'

'Ever the cheeky one!' she spat. 'Specially now you know I 'm goin'!'

I could see Mrs. Hudson restraining her sister gently by the arm. I bolted over the threshold and ended up outside on the pavement. I joined Holmes and the King.

'Phew! Thank goodness we are seeing the back of her!' I said, just as Holmes was finishing his explanation of why he kept the King's royal personage a secret from the two sisters and the King muttering something about Mrs. Turner being a victim of modern society. What claptrap!

We climbed aboard the King's brougham. My goodness me, this was luxury itself! The seats were deep cushions of velvet. The carpet was a lush lawn in the height of an English summer. The lamps were crystal leaded lights of tinkling clarity wrapped in ornate, wrought silver, and when the door was closed with an inoffensively dull thunk! We were thrust into our own silent world. When we started off once more for Briony Lodge the movement was so smooth it was like surfing on mercury; I hardly noticed the setting off. As we sank down into our seats, adjusted our undercarriage and settled down, Holmes sensed the time was right to introduce our client to the latest news.

'Irene Adler is married,' remarked Holmes.

'Married! When?'

'Yesterday.'

'But to whom?'

'To an English chap named Norton.'

'Not Graham?'

'No, Godfrey, a lawyer.'

'But she could not love him?'

'I am in hopes that she does.'

'And why in hopes?'

'Because it would spare Your Majesty all fear of future annoyance. If the lady loves her husband, she does not love your Majesty. If she does not love Your Majesty, there is no reason why she should interfere with Your Majesty's plan.'

'That is true, but I still wonder....Well, surely she could still love me?'

Holmes flashed his eyes over at me and then stared back at the King with an enquiring incline of his noble head. His Majesty received the message loud and clear.

'Well, I suppose she may be able to fall in love with another man, but such a thing I had neffer imagined before in my life. I just wish that she had been of my own station. What a queen she would haff made!'

He relapsed into a moody silence, as he was undoubtedly reflecting on the good times that he had spent with her, and, then, the sad realisation that a wretched lawyer would be taking his place. A lawyer, no less! As I gazed at the King staring sulkily out of the window, the devil, I thought, don't these kings have it all their own way? I have to confess that I felt a twinge of jealously towards our client as I imagined the gorgeous, fabulous Irene Adler in his clutches, in the throes of joy and laughter, and then joined it to the vision of how Clotilde Lothman von Saxe-Meningen might look on her wedding night, which was an evocation of the erotic image that the King had showed us. Talk about riding a cock horse to Banbury Cross! How could he be so selfish? I switched my gaze across to the great detective, whose nod of his head told me that he was thinking the same. The King dwelt upon his loss, like a spoiled child, until we drew up in Serpentine Avenue.

The door of Briony Lodge was open, and an elderly woman stood upon the steps. She watched us with a sardonic eye as we stepped from the brougham.

'Mister Sherlock Holmes, I believe?' she said.

'I am Mr. Holmes,' answered my companion, looking at her with a questioning and rather startled gaze.

'Indeed! My mistress told me that you were likely to call. She left this morning with her husband, by the 5.15 train from Charing Cross, for the Continent.'

'Never!' Sherlock Holmes staggered back, white with chagrin and surprise. 'Do you mean that she has left England?'

The messenger's eyes sprung to life by Holmes's animated shock. 'Yes, young man! Never to return!' crowed the old bag triumphantly.

'And the papers?' asked the King hoarsely. 'All is lost!'

The elderly woman chuckled to herself, the adjutant relishing her duty set by her General. She was no doubt itching to deliver an account of this scene to Irene Adler later on, somewhere "on the Continent."

'We shall see!' Holmes pushed past the jolly servant, and rushed into the drawing room, followed by the King. I was in their wake until I had to stop myself for a medical emergency. Did Holmes mean to tread on the servant's toes as he rushed by? No, I am sure he did not, but I made a hesitant enquiry as to her wellbeing, principally to try and calm her down and stop her from shouting: 'MY ARTHRITIS, YOU BASTARD!'

The furniture in the drawing room was scattered about in every direction, with dismantled shelves and open drawers, as if the lady had hurriedly ransacked them before her flight. When I arrived in the room Holmes had rushed to the bell-push and he was tearing back a small sliding shutter, and, plunging in his hand, pulled out a photograph and a letter. The photograph was of Irene Adler herself looking resplendent in evening dress, looking the letter was superscribed to "Sherlock Holmes, Esq. To be left until called for." My friend tore it open, and he read it out to the three of us together.

'This is dated midnight of the preceding night, and runs in this way:

"MY DEAR MR. SHERLOCK HOLMES. You really did it very well. You took me in completely. Until after the alarm of the fire, I had no suspicion. But then, when I found how I had betrayed myself, I began to think. I had been warned against you months ago. I had been told that if the King employed an agent, it would certainly be you. And your address had been given to me. Yet, with all this, you made me reveal what you wanted to know. Even after I became suspicious, I found it hard to think evil of such a dear, kind old clergyman. But, you know, I have been trained as an actress myself. Male costume is nothing new to me. I often take advantage of the freedom which it gives. I sent John, the coachman, to watch you, ran upstairs, got into my walking clothes, as I call them, and came down just as you departed.

Well, I followed you to your door. That meant stopping off and wait for you at The Dog & Duck Then, The Three Crowns. And, finally, The Duke of Cumberland."'

*Those who made fun of Sherlock Holmes
risked severe retribution.*

'What are these places?' enquired the King.

'Hostelries, Your Majesty, where warm ale and a good smoke can uncover many a fact of the matter to help solve a mystery.'

The King turned his head and looked me in the eyes. I nodded in agreement.

'Ignore him Your Majesty,' said Holmes.

The King acknowledged. Holmes continued.

'"I was forced to loiter in Kingly Street for three hours outside Mother Kelly..."'

'Who iss this Mother Kelly?' asked the King.

'It's an upmarket knocking-shop, Your Majesty,' I quipped.

'Ignore him!' cried Holmes.

'*Ja,* I know, ignore him!' crowed the King, and then laughed himself pink. 'But I haff heard of this place, with many fine women. *Ja*?' Holmes nodded and removed a fountain pen from his breast pocket.

'Anyway, she crossed that out...' He crossed out the text furiously... 'No, I cannot make head nor tail...Ah yes, she picks it up here again... "I followed you to your door in Baker Street. Then, to make sure that I was really an object of interest to the celebrated Mr. Sherlock Holmes, I rather imprudently wished you good night, and started for the Temple to see my husband.

'We both thought the best resource was to flight when pursued by such a formidable antagonist; so you will find the nest empty when you call tomorrow. As to the photograph, your client may rest in peace. I love and am loved by a better man than he. The King may do what he will without hindrance from one who he has cruelly wronged. I keep it only to safeguard myself, and to preserve a weapon which will always secure me from any steps which he might take in the future. And, besides, I wish to have an image of Merkel to remind me of our happy days together. I leave this photograph which he might care to possess; and I remain, dear Mr. Sherlock Holmes, very truly yours,

   IRENE NORTON, née ADLER."'

'What a woman! Oh, what a woman!' cried the King of Bohemia. 'Did I not tell you how quick and resolute she was? Would she not have made an admirable queen? Iss it not a pity she was not on my level?'

'From what I have seen of the lady, she seems, indeed, to be on a very different level to Your Majesty,' said Holmes coldly. 'I am sorry that I have not been able to bring Your Majesty's business to a more successful conclusion.'

'On the contrary, my dear sir,' cried the King. 'Nussing could be more successful. I know that her word iss inviolate. The photograph iss now as safe as if it were in the fire.'

'Well, if you don't mind me saying, Your Majesty, we have had our fair share of fires in this commission of yours.' said Holmes.

'But nothing could be more safe than the destruction of the offending article.' I added.

Holmes leaned forwards, about to speak, when the King put up his hand to stop him. 'I know, Herr Holmes, I must ignore him.'

'I am glad to hear Your Majesty say so.'

'Herr Holmes, I am immensely indebted to you. Pray tell me in what way I can re-vord you. Zis ring...'

He slipped an emerald snake ring from his finger and held it out upon the palm of his hand.' We both craned in our heads to take a closer look at it. Holmes picked it up and held it to the light. 'Hmmm!' he said. 'A very nice colour. And it seems to be flawless, although I would need a glass to be sure.'

He offered it to me. I took a look at it, but I was no expert on gems. It just looked green to me. I thought the snake setting was somewhat tasteless and maybe that showed up in my face as it was seized back by my friend.

'Your Majesty has something which I should value even more highly,' said Holmes as he returned the ring to the King.

'You haff but to name it.'

Ah, the old fox, I thought! He wants the brougham, and I cannot say that I blame him. She was a beauty.

'The photograph, please!'

The King stared at him in amazement.

'The Princess?'

'Quite so, Your Majesty.'

'Certainly! If you wish it.' And the King handed over the photograph. 'But keep it to yourself, Herr Holmes!

'I thank Your Majesty. Then there is no more to be done in this matter. I have the honour to wish you a very good morning.' He bowed, and, turning away without observing the hand which the King had stretched out to him, he set off for Baker Street. The King stared at Holmes for quite a while and then he turned to me. I was embarrassed about the way that my friend had behaved, and I made sure that I looked suitably so. I held out my hand to the King, who glanced down it with derision, and then I remembered about the protocol when in the presence of royalty and withdrew it.

'Your companion in the fighting of crime seems to be upset?' said the King.

'It is time now to ignore him, Your Majesty. He is prone to anxiety when he rides the troughs of his chosen profession. The fact that he could not deliver the precious cargo into your hand, personally, makes him a failure, in his eyes.'

'But in my eyes, Doctor, he is not a failure.'

'Good, because once Mr. Holmes has recovered from his pique, I know that in recognition of his excellent service to you and the country of Bohemia he would like to have the brougham.'

The King smiled. 'Ah yes, indeed, he is a man of excellent taste but, sadly, that is not in my gift. It is the property of the embassy.'

'Then would Your Majesty be comfortable with the ring plus, say, five thousand pounds?'

His Majesty smiled and held out his hand. I took it. I shook it.

'Actually, instead of pounds, could we make that five thousand guineas?'

* * *

And that was how a great scandal threatened to affect the kingdom of Bohemia; how the best plans of Mr. Sherlock Holmes were beaten by a woman's wit and charm; and how I got rid of my female-impersonator wife and still had two hundred and fifty pounds over.

Holmes used to make merry over the cleverness of women, but I have not heard him do it of late. When he speaks of Irene Adler, or when he refers to her photograph, it is always under the honourable title of *the* woman. And whenever we talk about my marriage contract with Mary Morstan, he still mentions his surprise that he/she settled upon forty pounds and a couple of old shirt buttons by giving me a look of comical disbelief. He may be the finest detective in the world, and I love him for it, but this simple ruse proved to me that he didn't know *everything!*